For Elizabeth, Hilary and Linda

A Dog
by any Other Name
is Not the Same

by J.G. Piper

Illustrated by
Linda Apple

The world is a place with many different dogs,
big, **tall**, little and **small**.

Some run fast and some not at **all**,

but most of them like to play with a **ball**.

The colors of dogs can vary **a lot**:

black or white and sometimes a **spot**.

Brown and cream are a popular **hair**,

a mix of both adds a little **flair**.

There are farm dogs and city dogs,
there are dogs all around.
You can find them herding cattle or
walking downtown.

Each dog is different in every case.
No dog has the same name,
that lives in the same place.

Every dog is special, just look in their face;
they all have their own story,
one to embrace.

My name is Charlie Chihuahua,
and I live on a farm.
I like to think of myself
as a good luck charm.

One day I saw a man I didn't know:
he was big and walked very slow.
I thought he might do us some harm,
so I ran and barked,
and sounded the alarm.

He then continued to walk along,
good thing I was there,
so nothing went wrong.

Apple

My name is Priscilla Pug.

People tell me I have a beautiful mug.

They say it's a face you have to adore,

but when I see myself, I'm really not sure.

When they look at me they seem to be happy.

I think they're just being a bit sappy.

I think I look more like an old wrinkled glove,

with a face that only a mother could love.

They look at me with such fondness that I don't see,

maybe I should try seeing myself,

the way they see me.

My name is Barry Boxer,

and I'm a dedicated watcher.

The best watchdog you will ever find:

brave, loyal and kind.

I've got many heroic stories to tell:

times where I made sure that all went well.

People have tried to bribe me with treats of ham.

I won't fall for it though, it's not who I am.

My name is Princess Poodle,

and I'm a pampered pooch.

You should feel lucky if I give you a smooch.

It's not often I give out my affection:

when you are royalty,

you need to do it with discretion.

I come from a noble and proper breed:

we're not ones to follow but rather lead.

Some people say I'm stubborn to a fault.

I say I can't help it, I'm just superior by default.

We are the three amigos:

Pedro, Paco and Pete,

the nicest brothers you

would ever want to meet.

We do everything together,

you'll never find us alone.

We like each other so much,

we'll even share a bone.

We play games together when we go to the park.

If we see other dogs,

we'll stand together and bark.

We cuddle when it's cold, and keep each other warm.

When the weather gets bad, we protect one another,

from scary sounds during the storm.

My name is **Lacey Lab.** I'll lay in the sun all day.

I prefer it to chasing down horses, or rolling in the hay.

You may think I'm a drowsy dog, sleeping the day away,

but I assure you that won't be the case when you say,

"get up Lacey, it's time to play."

My favorite is catching Frisbees as they fly through the sky.

I do it with style and jump really high.

Don't be confused and think sunbathing makes me lazy.

If I see a squirrel I'll be up fast,

and you'll see me run like crazy.

My name is Donny Dachshund,
  and I'm a city dog.
I live in a building so tall,
  it's sometimes in the fog.
I like to look out the window
  and watch the people and cars far below;
It's also fun at night,
  when the city is aglow.

It's an exciting place and everything moves fast,
  but I walk too slow and always get passed.
There are many different noises and lots to see,
  being a downtown dog is the right life for me.

My name is Bella Beagle,

and I'm having a relaxing day.

I'm tired from yesterday,

when I went out to the park to play.

Today is a day for lounging around,

I'll mosey here and there,
find a comfy spot

and sleep very sound.

I've scheduled naps all day,

with an occasional long yawn.

I'll sleep mostly in the house

but sometimes on the lawn.

Once in awhile it's nice to be a lazy dog,

taking it easy rather than going for a jog.

My name is Sam Scottie,

and Saturdays are my favorite day.

There's a farmers market not far away.

I like all the fruits and vegetables that people sell.
I like how they look

and the way that they smell.

I look at everyone's expressions
as they walk around

and ask each other questions.

There's hustle and bustle, and people all talk.

I think the market is the best place to walk.

My name is Bonnie Basset,

and I'm new to this place.

I get happy when I see a familiar face.

I'm a baby, only a few months old.

I haven't done a lot yet, truth be told.

My family is very loving:

always smiling and hugging.

Yesterday, something happened

that was very neat:

I sat and rolled over,

and they gave me a treat.

My name is Billy Bulldog,

and I live where it's warm all year round.

My folks miss the snow,

so they decided to clown around.

They dressed me like Santa for some holiday cheer.

I guess it's alright –

but they forgot my reindeer!

And while we're at this,

some presents would be nice.

How about a big dog bone,

if you want to be precise?

I'm happy to provide amusement for all,

but how about some elves to throw me my ball?

My name is Sophie Spaniel,

and I like to watch birds fly,

I enjoy seeing them do twirls high in the sky.

I like the sounds when they chirp and tweet.

I wish I could talk to the birds,

that would be so neat.

Sometimes I dream I'm a bird flying all around,

then I wake up and realize

I'm stuck on the ground.

People say I'm suppose to hunt the birds I marvel at,

but I'd rather just sit and watch them fly

this way and that.

My name is Colin Collie,

    and I don't like to be house bound.
I like to run through the fields
    and all around.

I was born to run fast and free;

    being confined inside is not for me.

I like the smell of apple blossoms in the open-air.

    To be stuck in a house, it's just not fair.

I'm a dog who likes every season;

    I just love being outside, I don't need a reason.

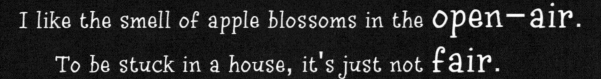

The sun is setting and
our dog stories all told.
Now you can see, dogs are very different
and don't fit one mold.
Running through a field or
or walking down a street.
The things dogs do,
are really pretty neat.

Puppies are young and jump all around;

joyous and fun, but hard to calm down.

Old dogs are wise and often sleepy;

content and happy, they dream very deeply.

Dogs can be sweet, loving and loyal;

those are the ones you can hug and spoil.

A dog can be called a pooch or a hound,

but we'd rather be called your best friend,

wherever we're found.

Visit us on the web at:
JGPiper.com and AppleArts.com

ISBN-13:
978-1530883882
ISBN-10:
1530883881

Made in the USA
Lexington, KY
13 December 2017